To my Student
Camille
Enjoy the Rainforest

Shirley Najuan

Layers of the Rainforest

-AN EDUCATIONAL JOURNEY-

by

Shirley Najhram

Tate Publishing, LLC.

Dedication

To my loving children

Nicholas and Cindy

Acknowledgment

With special thanks to my

dearest friend Girmalla Persaud

Foreword

Shirley Najhram has created a richly suggestive text to stir the imagination of her young readers. With persuasive simplicity she evokes the rhythm of rainforest life and crafts layers of new images for a child's mind.

In Guyana, South America, as a child raised in the warmth of a close family, Ms Najhram learned to love the rainforest the way her mother did. She left Guyana for England at eighteen when her mother died but returned with her children and shared the rainforest with her family.

This book was inspired by a child's memories and is so obviously the product of a mother's love. As an Early Childhood Educator of young children, Shirley Najhram brings to her work an understanding of and respect for the potential in a young child's mind.

Michael J. Sherman - Editor, ABLE Magazine

Fruit

Flower

One look at the rainforest,

nature at its best.

A shelter, home and food for animals I bet.

Oh! It is the best.

Food

Flower

Scarlet Macaw

Bee

One look at the beautiful broadleaved evergreens,

I see all colourful birds and insects among the leaves.

Animals and reptiles living in peace,

throughout the blooming rainforest trees.

Oh! Such beautiful trees!

Frog

Jaguar

Morpho Butterfly

Toco Toucan

One look at the top of the trees,

the emergent layer I see through the sunlight,

Colourful birds flying.

Oh! What a beautiful sight!

To see the noisy toco toucans with

their rainbow bright beaks.

Morpho butterflies fluttering from

flower to flower, nectar they seek.

Howler monkeys and spider monkeys chattering,

while the hummingbirds are flying.

Oh! Can you hear the buzzing bees?

Howler Monkey

Flower

Hummingbird

One look at the canopy,

Just below the emergent layer

Can it be?

The busiest part of the rainforest,

packed with colour, action and sounds.

In this beautiful rainforest I found

howler monkeys swinging

from branch to branch eating

flowers and fruits.

Hummingbirds flying around feeding on nectar,

while insects make musical sounds.

Oh! Such action all around!

Grasshopper

Tree Porcupine

Three-toed Sloth

Another look at the canopy,

Guess what I see?

A scarlet macaw, coloured so brightly

with extra strong beaks for cracking open nuts.

Tree porcupines hold onto branches with their strong

gripping tails.

It's a treat to see the three-toed sloth

hanging upside down and not in fear.

Look at the iguana!

Stretched out on a tree branch enjoying the sun.

Oh! What fun!

Scarlet Macaw

Iguana

Tree Boa

One look at the understory,

Just below the canopy,

Smaller trees, tangled vines, and climbing

plants that twine around the trees make up

this interesting layer.

The emerald tree boa snake and

tree frogs gripping on branches, and tangled vines

in their wake.

Oh! It's a glory!

Vine

Frog

Tapir

Jaguar

Termite

One look at the forest floor
home to large animals.
Giant anteaters rooting around
for plants and insects to eat.
Jaguars prowl through the jungle
in search of prey.
Tapirs rest in the shade
by the river during the day
and search for food at night.
Rotting branches and dead leaves
that fall from the trees are home for small creatures.
Ants, termites, and earthworms make their homes here.
Oh! I wish I could see more!

Anteater

Beetle

Ant

Another look at the forest floor,
you are sure to see the giant
armadillo digging for
worms and other creatures.
Oh! I am sure!

Armadillo

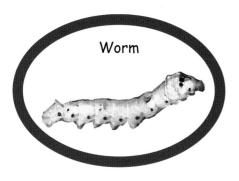

Worm

Parakeets

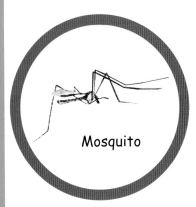
Mosquito

One look at the jungle river with all of its might.

To see the ripple in the water,

fishes swimming playfully.

Many other creatures live along

the riverbank.

Even the anaconda, the largest snake can be seen

slithering along

the riverbank.

Crocodiles live in the shallow water

waiting to catch birds and other animals.

Oh! I shiver at the sight!

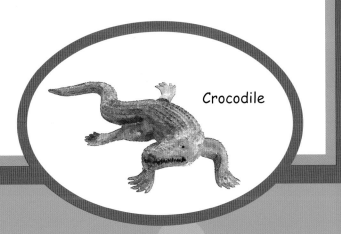
Crocodile

Moon

One look at the stream,

a reflection of the moon.

Shining over the giant water lilies.

These creamy coloured

flowers open at night.

Oh! What a dream!

Flower

Water Lilies

Bat

At night, bats and moths emerge.

By day, moths rest in the cracks

or crevices or among foliage.

The little pottos sleep in the trees

By day and hunt at night.

Oh! What a fright!

Potto

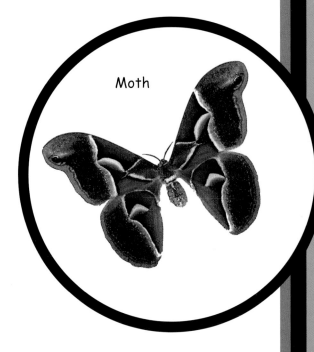
Moth

Bee

Insects carry pollen
from plant to plant
pollinating flowers.
Can you see the blossoms
of the beautiful flowers?
Oh! Something is crawling!

Flower and Butterfly

Ladybug

Fern

Fruit

One look at the plant life,

what a beautiful feeling

of being alive!

Rainforest trees are very tall,

broadleaved evergreens.

Ferns and mosses grow in

abundance.

Most of the colours in the rainforest

are provided by flowering

plants and fruits.

Oh! What a colourful life!

Moss

Flower

Monkey

Oh! Beautiful rainforest,

you are the best!

You give the animals food and a place to rest.

Your trees shelter the animals from

the radiant sun, the drizzling rain, and the strong wind.

Oh! Thank you nature for everything!

Frog

Food

Emergent Layer

Canopy Layer

Understory

Forest Floor

Glossary

Canopy Layer– Thick clumps of trees make up the canopy which is below the emergent layer. The canopy is a busy and noisy place.

Emergent Layer– The highest level of the rainforest that gets the most sunshine. The emergent layer is made of the tops of the tallest trees.

Forest Floor– Few plants grow because little sunlight reaches it. The forest floor is composed of leaf litter, twigs, fallen fruits and animal remains. Big animals stay on the forest floor.

Rainforest– is referred to as a jungle which is a Hindi word from India meaning "a wilderness".

Understory– This layer has small trees, bushes and vines which is beneath the canopy. It is very shady in this layer.

TATE PUBLISHING, LLC

Tate Publishing is committed to excellence in the publishing industry. Our staff of highly trained professionals—editors, graphic designers, and marketing personnel—work together to produce the very finest book products available. The company reflects in every aspect the philosophy established by the founders based on Psalms 68:11, "The Lord gave the word and great was the company of those who published it."

If you would like further information, please call
1.888.361.9473
or visit our website at
www.tatepublishing.com

Tate Publishing LLC
127 E. Trade Center Terrace
Mustang, Oklahoma 73064 USA